Milly's Tri

"**M**illy!" Neil called gently. He knew he had to get her indoors as soon as possible, but the little dog just darted to and fro in distress. Neil had almost got hold of her when a firework shot into the air with a crack so loud it hurt his ears, and Milly, with a whimper, ran off. Fuelled by terror, she sped across the garden, cleared the wall and raced across the road . . .

Puppy Patrol
Milly's Triumph

Jenny Dale

Illustrated by

Mick Reid

A Working Partners Book

MACMILLAN CHILDREN'S BOOKS

Special thanks to Margaret McAllister

First published 1999 by Macmillan Children's Books
a division of Macmillan Publishers Limited
25 Eccleston Place, London SW1W 9NF
Basingstoke and Oxford
www.macmillan.co.uk

Associated companies throughout the world

Created by Working Partners Limited
London W6 0QT

ISBN 0 330 39087 2

1 3 5 7 9 8 6 4 2

A CIP catalogue record for this book is available from
the British Library.

Typeset in Bookman Old Style by SX Composing DTP, Rayleigh, Essex
Printed and bound in Great Britain by Mackays of Chatham plc, Kent

Chapter One

Neil Parker jumped down from the green Range Rover onto the pavement outside the TV Rental shop on Compton High Street.

"Sorry, Jake," said Neil, reaching up to give his dog a farewell pat. "We can't take you in and out of every shop in Compton. You'll have to go home with Mum."

Jake looked at Neil with bright, intelligent eyes and barked.

Neil's younger sister, Emily, pushed a sheaf of posters into his arms before climbing down to join him. Five-year-old Sarah, the youngest of the Parker family, hung on tightly to the eager, tail-wagging Border collie.

"He can come with me to my ballet lesson if he likes," giggled Sarah.

Carole, their mother, laughed. "See you later," she said. "Best of luck with your poster campaign."

Moments later she drove away and left Neil looking admiringly at the pile of posters in his arms. "LOCK UP YOUR DOGS!" warned the bold caption. Underneath was added, "Fireworks are a pet's nightmare. Keep your dogs and cats indoors on Saturday." Against a background of exploding fireworks was a picture of a small terrier wearing a safety helmet and covering its ears with its paws. Neil and Emily had designed the poster on the office computer and were very proud of their work.

"Let's get a move on," said Emily. "We need to get all of these round Compton by the end of the evening."

It had been Emily's idea to produce the poster because Compton's annual firework display and bonfire in the park was due to take place the following evening. It would be noisy, fun and full of excitement for families, but for nervous animals it could be very dangerous. Neil and Emily were concerned that all pets should be kept safely at home that night.

The Parkers ran King Street Boarding Kennels and rescue centre, and for Neil, there was nothing in the world more important than dogs.

He took one more admiring glance at the poster. "Nice artwork, Em," he said. "OK, first stop, Mrs Smedley's shop. We'll start there, work our way along, and then do the other side."

At the end of the school day, Mrs Smedley's newsagent shop was always busy. When Neil and Emily walked in they found it full of their friends from Meadowbank School buying sweets and magazines.

Mrs Smedley took the poster with a nod and a smile. Then she turned with a concerned look towards Neil. "I heard about Sam, Neil," she said kindly. "I'm so sorry. He was such a fine dog."

Neil was never quite sure what to say when people asked about Sam, Jake's father. Sam had been a brilliant dog and Neil's special friend, and Neil found it hard to talk about his death. Sam had rescued Jake from drowning, but his own weak heart had failed from the effort of pulling Jake out of the water. Neil was still adjusting to life without him.

Neil nodded and muttered his thanks. Jake was growing into a fine young dog too now, but Neil still couldn't look at him without thinking of Sam. His friend Hasheem wandered over, bought some sweets and offered Neil a mint.

"Are you going round *all* the shops?" he asked.

"Yes, and to all the houses where people might put up posters. Then we're going to our kennel maid's house. Bev said we could go and meet Milly."

"Who's Milly?"

Before Neil could reply, a high-pitched and excited yapping erupted from nearby and caught everyone's attention. "I know that bark!" Emily grinned and ran out of the shop, nearly colliding with a woman in the doorway.

"Sorry, Mrs Sparrow!" she said. "I wanted to say hello to Scrap."

Outside, Toby Sparrow, who was in Emily's class at school, was hanging on with both hands to the lead of his bright and energetic young Dalmatian pup. Scrap's spotted coat was developing its glossy Dalmatian sheen, and he was bubbling over with energy and friendly enough to greet anyone.

"Down!" said Toby, as Scrap leapt up in

4

delight and pawed at Emily. "I'm waiting out here while Mum's in the shop. There's nothing to tie his lead to, but I don't mind holding on to him."

Scrap certainly looked as if he needed holding on to when he saw Neil. The dog pulled at his lead and danced his greeting all over again.

"Get down, Scrap!" said Emily, giving him a pat. "Here's a poster for your mum, Toby."

"If you must run a beauty parlour for dogs, you may as well have decent posters in it," said Neil, who couldn't resist teasing the Sparrow family about the Pretty Paws grooming parlour. "Come on, Em, we can't play with Scrap all evening."

"They said goodbye to Toby and set off, going in and out of several shops on the High Street to give out their posters. Then they turned left uphill to the smarter, residential part of Compton.

"I'm not looking forward to seeing the Jepsons again," grumbled Neil. "I'm glad they don't board Sugar and Spice at King Street any more."

"Me too," replied Emily. "But they're people we know, and they're dog owners."

"That's the trouble," muttered Neil. "Sugar and Spice – the Westie Pesties – and Mrs Jepson who thinks she's their Mumsy-Wumsy. Aaaargh!"

"All we have to do is leave a poster and go," said Emily, chuckling. "If all the people we know take posters for their window, nobody will forget dog awareness on Firework Night. Anyway, Mr Jepson's on the council, so he's a good person to have on our side."

"He hasn't got a clue about his dogs, though," muttered Neil. Walking up the Jepsons' garden path, they heard sustained and angry barking.

"Told you. Sugar and Spice are having a yapping practice already."

"Look, the Jepsons have got the builders in," said Emily. There were no workmen to be seen, but there was scaffolding around the house and piles of bricks covered in blue polythene sheeting were stacked against a wall. Mrs Jepson answered the door. She was dressed entirely in bright pink, and was carrying something that looked like a large cuddly toy. Then the cuddly toy growled. It was definitely one of the Jepsons' spoilt West Highland terriers – but they couldn't tell if it was Sugar or Spice.

"We've just come to give you a poster," said Emily quickly. "Will you put it up in your window, please?"

Mrs Jepson took it without a smile. "I've got such a headache," she complained. "The builders are working on our extension, and they've been drilling and hammering all day. It upsets the poor dogs terribly and they won't stop barking. It's because they're so sensitive. Their nerves must be in shreds, poor little poppets. I know mine are."

Neil and Emily departed as quickly as they could before their giggles overcame them.

"That's everyone except Bev," said Neil. "And Milly."

Until recently, the Parker family had run King Street Kennels with only one kennel maid – the hard-working and dedicated Kate McGuire – to help them, but now the kennels had expanded, Bev had been taken on as their new member of staff. She was naturally gifted with animals, and Neil and Emily had been dying to meet her own dog, Milly, who had once been a King Street dog herself.

"Bev said her husband would take some posters to work with him," said Emily. "And her son, Andrew, is going to take some to work too.

It's the next house on the left. I hope she—"

"Sshh!" said Neil sharply. "Listen!"

They both stopped. Neil and Emily glanced at each other in concern as they heard it again – a confusion of snapping and snarling and yelping. It was the unmistakable sound of very angry dogs.

"This way!" Neil ran full pelt towards the noise, with Emily close on his heels.

"I don't believe it," he panted, slowing down. "It's those two!"

"Which two?" gasped Emily. "Oh!"

On the nearest front garden path, two furious dogs were growling and springing at each other. Both were well known at King Street. Pooh-Bah, a Pekinese, snarled, snapped and bristled as he circled Bernie, a slow-moving and slower-thinking St Bernard, who squared up to the Peke with a deep and threatening growl. With a snarl, Pooh-Bah sprang at Bernie, who lurched forward and thundered into his flank – then the two of them began brawling on the pavement like street fighters.

Neil surged forward. "C'mon, Em. We've got to stop them!"

Chapter Two

"Pooh-Bah! Bernie! Leave it!" ordered Neil. The fierce-faced Peke and the enormous St Bernard checked themselves for a moment and looked at him – but then Pooh-Bah started snapping at Bernie. The St Bernard stood his ground and growled menacingly.

Dan, the Peke's owner, was running from the nearest house.

"Stand back!" he shouted. "I'll deal with it!"

"No, don't! Wait!" yelled Neil, and ran through the open front door. "I've got an idea!" He quickly found the kitchen, filled a bowl with water from the sink, and ran back outside with water sloshing out over the sides. With a well-aimed heave he threw it over the dogs.

The shock made them separate long enough for Neil to grab Bernie's collar and hang on to it with both hands. Dan lunged forward and got a grip on his startled Peke as it shook water from its drenched coat.

Then the St Bernard's owner joined them with a lead in his hand. His hair was white and receding, but he sprinted up the path like an athlete and soon had the dripping Bernie under control. Neil and Emily recognized John Cartwright, who had boarded Bernie at King Street one Christmas.

"What are we going to do with the pair of them, Dan?" called John Cartwright over his shoulder. He steered Bernie down the path into the house next door and shut him in. He came back brushing loose tufts of hair from his trousers.

"Do they always fight?" asked Neil.

Dan shrugged. "I don't understand it. Pooh-Bah's always been all right with other dogs until now. He hates cats, but he's never taken against another dog, not while I've had him."

"And we've had Bernie at King Street before," said Emily. "He's bombproof."

"Yes, I remember you two. Neil and Emily,

isn't it?" said John Cartwright. "You know, I used to train mountain rescue dogs so I've sorted out a lot of doggy problems over the years, but this is beyond me. You know what Bernie's like. Dopiest dog I've ever met. He didn't bother at all when Pooh-Bah first moved in next door, but now they hate each other."

"Not easily provoked, is he?" agreed Dan, and frowned at his own dog. "I think it's Pooh-Bah's fault. He just keeps trying to attack Bernie."

"Has he been doing anything else out of character?" asked Neil.

"Yes, as a matter of fact – but just in the last week or so. He's been scratching away at the bottom of the fence, trying to get into John's garden, which is something he's never done before. Of course, Bernie defends his territory and sees him off. You'd think Pooh-Bah did it on purpose, to be annoying. And there's been a bit of snapping and growling up to now, but never anything like this."

Neil knelt beside the Peke, talking gently to calm him down. Pooh-Bah had a long, silky coat and a pedigree, and usually looked as if he knew it. Now, however, he looked more like a soaking wet, oversized rat. Subdued, he sniffed cautiously at Neil before there was a nervous wag of the tail and a lick of the hand.

"I'll mention it to Dad," said Neil, brushing loose earth and dust from Pooh-Bah's coat. "There's always a reason for unusual doggy behaviour – you just have to find out what it is."

"Hi, everyone! I came out to see what the racket was about." A small woman with neat fair hair had come to join them. She wore dark jeans and a sweatshirt with a picture of a Labrador on the front.

"Hi, Bev!" said Neil with a smile. "We were on our way to see you and Milly!"

"That's my house, further along the street.

The one with the you-know-what on the doorstep, if you want to come over."

Neil and Emily looked, and saw a tortoise-shell cat sitting upright on the step. Evidently cats were not to be mentioned in front of Pooh-Bah.

"I'll get him indoors before he sees it," said Dan. "He's in enough trouble for one day as it is. Away you go, the pair of you, and meet Milly. Now, there's a dog with a bit of sense."

They said goodbye to John and Dan, then hurried across the road to the small, warmly-lit house where the tortoiseshell cat was sitting on the doorstep. She scampered in as soon as the door was opened, and they were greeted by the sound of barking.

"Shush, Milly, it's only us!" said Bev, opening the sitting room door. "Here she is!" And out came a dark, bright-eyed mongrel, sniffing busily round their ankles, wagging her tail, and reaching up to put her paws on Neil's knees.

"Down, Milly!" ordered Bev. Milly sat at once, her tail still wagging, her deep brown eyes fixed brightly on Bev's face. "Good girl!"

Milly was mostly black, with tan patches on her legs and chest and around her muzzle. Her coat was soft and thick, and her neat triangular ears were pricked to attention. There was an alert look about her as she sat and offered Neil a paw. Neil stroked her. She almost seemed to be smiling.

"Where're your manners, Milly?" said Bev. "Don't keep your guests in the hall. Come on in. Andrew's putting the kettle on. Mind you don't trip over the cat, she's always under everyone's feet."

The cat, however, was already curled up by the fire, and Neil and Emily sat on the floor with Milly. Neil ruffled her ears and smoothed the coat along her back.

"She's wonderful," said Neil.

"And isn't she good!" said Emily. "She's so well-behaved and gentle."

Bev's eye's shone with pride. "She's good at obedience too. I'm going to enter her into the Compton Show later this month. I'll smarten her up before then – she's also moulting every-where!" Bev brushed loose hairs from her sweater.

"So's the cat," said Neil, pointing.

"I didn't even know you had a cat, Bev," said Emily.

"That's Steppy," said Bev. "I found her in a box on the doorstep three years ago, when she was only a kitten. Whoever left her must have known that I liked animals. I wasn't sure what Milly would think of her, but I should have known."

She smiled fondly at Milly, who had rolled over to lean against Neil and have her tummy tickled.

"What was Milly like with her?" asked Neil.

"She loved her. Mothered her, licked her clean, curled up to sleep beside her, treated her like her own puppy."

Milly stood up, gave herself a shake, and disappeared behind the settee. She came back carrying a worn and rather grubby teddy bear, which she dropped at Neil's feet.

"She likes you," said Bev. "She's brought you her Christmas Bear. It's her favourite toy."

Neil lobbed the threadbare toy towards Emily and reached out for it as Milly quickly brought it back. "She was a King Street dog, wasn't she?"

"She certainly was," said Bev, as a dark-haired young man brought in a tray of tea and biscuits. Milly watched him eagerly, sitting perfectly still as he reached into his pocket and pulled out a dog treat. She was clearly very well trained.

"Thanks, Andrew," said Bev. She introduced Neil and Emily to her son, then told them Milly's story.

"When Milly was a pup, she belonged to a family with small children, and they didn't have a clue about dogs. The kids were allowed to climb on her, pull her tail, tease her, anything – they just treated her like a toy, and nobody stopped them."

"Oh, poor Milly!" Emily said.

"How can anyone let their kids do that?" demanded Neil. "It's not as if they can't learn. We all knew we had to be gentle with animals before we could even walk."

"I can remember Mum teaching Sarah to stroke Sam's hair in the right direction," said Emily.

"Well, this lot got tired of Milly when they had more interesting toys," said Bev. "Nobody had time for her any more. Sometimes she got a walk, sometimes she was just pushed into the yard and if the gate was open she roamed the streets, until one of the neighbours persuaded them that they shouldn't have got a dog in the first place. It was only when they got bored with her that they agreed to take her to the RSPCA."

"Why didn't they bring her to the King Street

17

rescue centre?" asked Neil, stroking Milly.

"You would have been very small," said Bev. "That was eight years ago, before your dad started it up. Anyway, she wasn't with the RSPCA long. She was adopted by a lady called Betty Cooke. She's still around. She's a retired lecturer, very clever – a widow with no family who wanted a companion. Milly was with her for five years, and they thought the world of each other. Betty must have had a lot to do with training her. Milly's a well-balanced dog, in spite of a bad start in life."

"Betty must have done her a lot of good," said Emily.

"Yes, she's a great personality, aren't you, Milly?" said Neil. "So then what happened, Bev? How come you came to be with her?"

"Well, Betty's neighbours heard Milly barking very early one morning, and she went on making a racket, which wasn't like her. They knew something must be wrong, so they tried ringing the doorbell and phoning, but there was no answer, so eventually they called the police and an ambulance."

"What did they find?" asked Emily.

"Betty was lying on the bedroom floor. She'd had a stroke, so she couldn't move and could barely speak. Milly was running backwards and forwards, barking for help then going back to nuzzle her and lick her. She kept her warm, and quite possibly kept her alive."

"I remember! I've heard that story before!" exclaimed Neil. "I didn't realize it was Milly!"

"Betty recovered, but she had to go into sheltered accommodation after that. She can't keep a dog there and she knew she couldn't cope with one, anyway. She needs a walking stick now so there are no more long walks."

"So Milly came to King Street," said Neil.

"Briefly. Betty was really upset, not knowing what would happen to her. She begged your parents to find her a good home."

"That must have been so difficult for her," said Neil, but he smiled as Milly rolled over against him again.

"Fortunately, it was at the exact time I was looking for a new dog. Our last dog, Scott, had died after thirteen years, and I just had to get another one. Andrew and I went to King Street, saw Milly, and she's been here ever since."

"And she still visits Betty," added Andrew.

"Oh, yes," said Bev. "I take her there every week. It's very important to both of them. Betty trained her brilliantly."

"Watch this," said Andrew. "Milly! Find the hairbrush!"

Milly trotted from the room, her identity tag jangling against her collar. When she came back, she carried a wooden hairbrush in her mouth, laid it at Andrew's feet, and sat proudly back.

"Well done!" said Andrew, giving her a pat. "She knows where everything is."

"Milly!" said Bev. "Find my purse!"

Milly knew where to look for that, too. As Neil and Emily watched, fascinated, Milly sniffed about, found Bev's handbag hanging on the

back of a chair, and gently lifted out the leather purse.

"Obedience is a game to her," said Bev, patting Milly proudly. "She should do well at the Compton Show."

The bright little dog had won Neil's heart. "Bev, can I do a feature about her on our website? She's a King Street success story."

"I don't see why not," said Bev. "Do you want to be famous, Milly?"

Emily glanced at her watch. "We'll have to go," she said. "It's a long way home."

"Don't forget to leave those posters," said Bev. "And as for you, Mrs Superdog," she said to Milly, "you can take a good look at them. There's absolutely no way you're going out tomorrow night. The display is just round the corner and you don't like fireworks one bit."

"Dogs never do," said Neil. "If you like, Mike Turner can give her a mild sedative. That way, she'll just crash out and snore until it's all over. Bye, Bev."

"She's a great dog, isn't she, Em?" said Neil to Emily as they walked back to King Street.

"Yes. She's so loyal," said Emily."

"And *intelligent* too. Like Sam was," he added.

"That must be why you like her so much," said Emily, smiling.

Perhaps that was true. Neil quickened his step, thinking of Jake, waiting and looking out for him at home. He would be watching the door, keen and hopeful, just as Sam had always been.

Chapter Three

"Mum, my wellies are too tight!" insisted Sarah. She sat on the kitchen floor at King Street, wriggling and twisting as she tried to squeeze her foot into a bright blue boot. "They hurt. I don't want to wear them to the bonfire party!"

"Wear my old ones," said Emily. "They're in the cupboard under the stairs. Put some thick socks inside them. Neil, are you coming?"

Sarah dashed upstairs. Neil, who had just written up Milly's story on the King Street Kennels website and was feeling rather pleased with himself, put on his warm jacket. He knelt down to make a fuss of Jake, who, having seen

Neil getting ready to go out, was jumping about with excitement.

"Sorry, Jake," he said, patting the wriggling bundle of fur. "You're going to have to stay in *again* today. Haven't you read the posters?"

Just then, Kate, the kennel maid, came in, followed by Neil and Emily's father, Bob Parker. He was a large, dark-haired, bearded man with a big smile. A draught of cold air came in with them through the open door.

"You need all your winter things on tonight," said Kate. "It'll be cold in the park. Are you ready?"

Sarah clumped downstairs with a pair of thick socks in one hand and a hamster cage in the other. She sat on the stairs, pulled on her socks, and dived into the cupboard to find Emily's old wellies.

"Mum," she called, "can I leave Fudge downstairs? He might be frightened of the fireworks if he's left alone up in my room."

Carole Parker gave a smile which Neil and Emily could see, and Sarah couldn't. Neil grinned. He knew that fireworks in the park weren't likely to disturb a hamster at the other end of Compton, especially one as placid as Fudge.

"Yes, Sarah, love," said Carole, raising an eyebrow at Neil. "I'll make sure he doesn't get scared. Oh, and that reminds me – can you call at Bev's on the way there?"

"Sure thing!" Neil looked up. "Any excuse to see Milly again!" He gently detached Jake from Sarah's old boots, which the puppy seemed to have decided were a new toy.

"Bev called at Mike's surgery this morning," said Bob. Mike was the local vet, and held Saturday morning surgeries at King Street. "She bought a sedative for Milly, as you suggested, but I've just found it in the office. She must have left it there and forgotten about it."

"We'd better go there first, then, and quickly," said Neil. He stuffed the small envelope into his pocket. "If Milly doesn't take it soon, it won't have time to work until it's too late."

"Come on, then," said Kate. "First stop, Bev's. Then Milly can have a quiet evening."

After they had been dropped off in town, Neil, Emily, Sarah and Kate walked hurriedly through the chilly night, joining the clusters of adults and children heading for the park. From a long way off they could see the orange beacon of leaping firelight against the night sky. The firework display had not yet begun, but bangs, pops and fizzes came from the streets and the surrounding gardens.

"People must be having their own firework parties in their back gardens," said Kate. "I bet they won't be as good as the one in the park."

"Look!" Sarah pointed as, high above them, a gold flame shattered into sparks. Another exploded in a rain of silver, and Sarah's eyes shone with delight.

"Tell you what, Squirt," said Neil, "you and Kate go straight to the park and see the fireworks. Emily and I will go to Bev's and catch up with you. We won't be long, it's almost opposite the park gate."

Kate nodded in agreement and Sarah grabbed her hand and dragged her eagerly to the nearest zebra crossing as Neil and Emily made their way to Bev's house.

"It's a bit dark along this road," remarked Emily. "These street lights must be broken."

The front door was wide open when they reached Bev's gate and the light from the hall lit the path, where a car was parked with the boot open. Andrew was bending over it, unloading cardboard boxes onto the pavement.

"Oh, it's you two!" he said with a smile. "We've just bought a new stereo system."

Neil was about to help him carry it in when they heard Bev calling from inside the house.

"Someone shut the sitting room door, please," she was saying, "or the front door, or both, or – oh, forget it, I'll do it myself."

"Too late!" said Emily, because Milly had already slipped out of the house. She was running across the garden to greet them.

"Here, Milly!" called Neil, patting his knees, and Milly bounded towards him just as a deafening racket of exploding fireworks came from a neighbouring garden. Milly shrank back and retreated a few steps, glancing from side to side.

"Milly!" Neil called gently. He knew he had to get her indoors as soon as possible, but the little dog just darted to and fro in distress. Neil had almost got hold of her when a firework shot into the air with a crack so loud it hurt his ears, and Milly, with a whimper, ran off. Fuelled by terror, she sped across the garden, cleared the wall and raced across the road.

Neil, Emily and Bev tore after her, but Milly was already far ahead and, in the darkness, she was soon out of sight. Breathless, they ran back to the house to find Andrew locking the front door.

"I'll take the car," he said, "I'll drive around and see if there's any sign of her in the streets. I'm really sorry about this, Mum."

"It's my fault, not yours," said Bev, and she turned to Neil and Emily. "She'll be so scared by now that she may not know where she's going, but there's just a chance she might find her way to Betty's. I'll leave a note for my husband to stay here in case she comes back then I'll go there first. It's not far."

"We'll search the park," said Neil. "Come on, Em."

Ignoring the firework display, which was now in full swing, they worked their way round the park, calling Milly's name between explosions of fireworks. They followed every path, climbed the banks to look in the hedges and peered over the bridge, but there was no sign of Milly.

"We can try the crowds around the bonfire," said Emily. Neil heard the anxiety in her voice. "She might look for human company."

"Let's try it, then," said Neil. "We'll ask around in case anyone's seen her."

The bangs grew louder as Neil and Emily ran

towards the crowds. The fire crackled and plumes of coloured smoke fizzed into the air with a smell of gunpowder.

"If Milly's here, she'll be terrified," muttered Neil.

"There's Toby and Amanda!" said Emily. "They might have spotted her."

They pushed through the crowd to where the Sparrows were watching the fireworks.

"It's a good bonfire, isn't it?" said Toby Sparrow.

"Bev's dog's run away," said Neil quickly. "A black and tan mongrel. Have you seen her?"

Amanda and Toby both nodded, seeing the concern in their faces.

"There was a dog running along beside the railings," Toby said.

"I called it, but it wouldn't come," added Amanda.

"We lost sight of it. It looked really scared."

"When was that?" demanded Neil, looking round.

"Five, maybe ten minutes ago," Toby said, frowning as he tried to remember.

"Which railings? Which way?" asked Neil.

Amanda pointed towards the main road.

"She could be trying to get home," said Emily, as they ran off, calling and calling for Milly. But there was still no sign of her.

"Five or ten minutes," said Emily. "She could be anywhere by now."

"Look!" said Neil. "By the gate!"

They couldn't be quite sure what they were looking at, but something was moving in the shadows. Neil put out a hand to stop Emily before she could run.

"Walk," he said. "We're tearing about after her, but she's already terrified. If we run now, so will she." Then he added, "It would help if those street lights were working."

"I think it's her," whispered Emily as they quietly drew closer. "Oh, I've lost her again now, she's disappeared into the hedge. No, there she is – Milly! Milly, come on! Good girl!"

A firework lit up the sky and, for a moment, they saw her clearly, her golden-brown patches catching the light. She lifted her head, but retreated a few steps. Her ears were pricked, and she was panting.

"She's still frightened," said Neil. "At least she's just inching away now, not running for it. If she could only hear Bev's voice, she'd probably be all right."

"That's not much use when Bev's at Betty's," said Emily.

"Come on, Milly," said Neil gently, but his voice was lost among the patter of fireworks shooting into the air. He crouched down to be nearer her level, aware that a car was parking opposite the gates, and the driver was getting out.

"There's Andrew," said Emily. "She might go to him, but I think he's got more sense than to call her from the other side of the road." Somewhere a firework exploded, and Milly shrank back with fear.

"It's all right, Milly," coaxed Neil. "Good girl, you're all right."

Behind them, the firework display was

working up to its dazzling finale. Neil stretched out his hands to Milly. She didn't come to him, but she didn't back away, either. The dog stood shivering and nervous, her tail tucked in.

Behind them a sudden storm of explosions crashed into the sky causing Milly to flee through the gates and onto the main road. Neil caught sight of Bev running towards the park from the street corner. Then there was a roar of engine noise, and a car came between Bev and the park.

"Milly!" yelled Neil. "Milly! Come here!"

Brakes screeched. A yelp of pain cut the air, and the bitter smell of burning tyres mingled with the smoke. Neil ran. Through the storm of fireworks and the banging of car doors, he heard Bev scream.

Chapter Four

Bev dashed across the road as the car door banged, calling Milly's name. Neil heard a man's voice, urgent and anxious.

"I just didn't see her! I didn't see her . . . I couldn't stop!"

Neil was already beside the car driver, a short young man, who was kneeling in the road with Milly. Bev was there too, cradling Milly's head in her lap, fondling her ears, her hands shaking. Milly whimpered softly. Her breathing was heavy, and her eyes were turned to Bev's face.

"I'm so sorry!" said the driver. "She seemed to come out of nowhere!"

Milly struggled to get up, but she yelped with pain and fell back into Bev's comforting hands.

"We need Mike," said Neil. "We'll go straight to the surgery. Sshh, sshh, Milly, you're going to be all right."

But he wasn't at all sure of that. Milly's left hind leg, bloodied and grazed, lay at an awkward angle, and the force of the car must have bruised her terribly. He knew that internal injuries were the biggest potential threat to her life.

"Will there be anyone at the vet's at this time of night?" asked the driver.

"There's always an emergency vet on call," said Neil. "With any luck, it'll be Mike. We'll have to move her very gently."

"Let me drive you there. I really feel I should help," the man said.

A crowd of onlookers had gathered. Neil could hear Sarah asking what was happening, and whether a dog had been killed.

Kate was shouldering her way through the crowd. "Stay here with Toby and Amanda for now, Sarah, while I see what I can do." She joined the little group around Milly.

"What's happened, is she . . . Bev!" She saw the strain on Bev's face. "Bev, is this your dog?"

"My dog and my fault," muttered Bev. Very lightly she placed her hand on the dog's chest and abdomen, checking for injuries. "Help me get her in the car. She needs careful handling. Ideally she shouldn't be moved at all, but I need to get her to Mike. Andrew, go and fetch her basket so we can keep her as flat as possible."

Moments later, very gently, they eased Milly into it. Bev took off her jacket and gently tucked it round the little dog before they lifted her into the car. However careful they were, Milly still whimpered and tried to struggle before she eventually lay back and gave in to the pain. Bev was biting her lip. Her voice was high-pitched and tearful as she tried to comfort Milly, though she needed comforting herself.

"I can see Milly's in good hands," said Kate as Neil, Emily and Bev got into the car. "I'll stay with Sarah and phone ahead to let the vet know you're on your way. If I get back to King Street before you, I'll tell them what's happened."

The driver was already revving the engine. "Which way to the vet's?"

Neil gave directions and they drove swiftly through the dark night to the surgery. Fireworks glittered occasionally in the sky around them, but there was no more thought of

35

bonfire parties. Neil and Emily sat quiet and anxious in the back of the car, and the only sounds were Bev's reassuring voice, and Milly's soft whimpers.

"This is it," said Neil. "There's a light on – yes, I can see Mike. It must be his night on duty."

The driver parked as near to the doors as he could, got out of the car and held the door for Bev and Milly. Mike hurried to meet them and listened to the hasty, anxious explanations.

"It's my fault," said the driver. "I didn't see her, I—"

"No, it's completely my fault," said Bev bitterly. "I left the sitting room door open, and—"

"Never mind that," said Mike briskly. "Let's get her on the table and I'll give her something for the pain and shock. Then I'll examine her. Before I do that, Bev, is she on any other medication?" Then he looked puzzled, and looked again at Milly's face. "Didn't she have a sedative tonight?"

"Oh!" Neil saw the flash of memory cross Bev's face. "I'd forgotten all about that!" she cried. "If only she'd had it – I can't even remember what I did with it!"

"I was bringing it to you," said Neil. "You'd left

it at King Street. I just didn't get it to you in time." He stood tensed in the doorway of the small consulting room as Mike lifted the stained jacket. Blood was darkening on Milly's leg, and her coat was matted. Milly, still panting, lay on her side, craning her neck to gaze up at Bev. She made a brave attempt to sit up and lick the blood from her gashed leg, but she soon fell back, weakened and defeated.

"I don't deserve you," whispered Bev, looking into Milly's eyes. "I'm so, so sorry, my Milly."

Then Mike closed the door, and there was nothing to do but wait.

Neil joined Emily in the waiting room and found her nervously biting at her fingernails. The driver was still there.

"There's no need for you to stay," Emily told him gently.

"Oh, there is." His face was tight with concern. "I want to know what happens. I've never had an accident before. She's a beautiful little creature. It's a good thing you were all there, you seem to be pretty clued up about dogs."

Neil didn't feel like talking, even about his favourite subject, but Emily explained about King Street. After a long time – Neil didn't know how long, but it seemed that Mike must be having a real struggle to save Milly – Bev came out from the consulting room. She sat down heavily, and hid her face in her hands. Emily, who by now was biting her nails again, stopped, and took Bev's shaking hand.

"How is she?"

Bev tried to speak, but couldn't. The consulting room door opened and Mike came out, drying his hands.

"You can see her now, if you want to," he said quietly to Neil and Emily. "Be very quiet, don't disturb her. She's not in any pain, but she must rest."

They stood in the scrubbed consulting room with its tang of disinfectant, and looked down at the dog stretched limply on the table. The anaesthetic Mike had given her had left her drowsy, and she lay peacefully with half-closed eyes, responding to no one. The injured leg had been cleaned and dressed, but Neil grimaced when he looked at it.

"Will she get through?" he asked.

"There are no life-threatening injuries," said Mike gravely, "but the leg is broken as well as badly gashed." Very gently he stroked the top of Milly's head, but there was no response. "This old girl is staying with me for a while, I'm afraid. I want to keep her under observation for at least two days, until I see if the leg's going to mend. I've set it, but I'm not hopeful at all. Even in a younger dog, it might not knit together."

"Of all the nights in the year to leave the door open!" muttered Bev. "I shouldn't be allowed to keep a dog. If I'd remembered the sedative, she would have been too drowsy to run away. If I'd checked the doors . . ."

"These things happen, Bev," said Mike. "Now, how are you getting home?"

"I'll take you home," offered the driver, who had anxiously followed them into the consulting room. "My name's Sean, by the way. Sean Appleby." He handed a business card to Mike, and Neil could see his name printed beneath the name of an advertising agency.

"I don't want to go home." Bev dried her eyes on a tissue. "I want to stay with her."

"Stay just a bit longer, then," said Mike. "But she needs peace and quiet, so . . ."

"Why don't I take you two home, and come back for Bev?" said Sean.

Neil looked at Emily. He could see that she felt as he did. They didn't really want to be with anyone else but it was probably best to get

home. "Thanks," he said. "And thanks for helping with Milly."

They left the surgery and drove back to King Street Kennels in silence.

Opening their own front door was like entering another world. Jake leapt up to meet them, jumping and wagging his tail with joy. Neil bent to rub his face against the warm, squirming fur, taking comfort in Jake's welcome.

Bob appeared, his face kind and concerned. "Your Mum's putting Sarah to bed," he said. "Kate brought her home and told us what happened. How's Milly?"

Neil and Emily told him what had happened at the surgery while he made tea and listened sympathetically. Now and again, he nodded with understanding. "There's nothing to do but wait now," he said. "It's a good thing you were all on the scene and that the driver was so helpful. She's alive and that's the main thing."

A ring at the doorbell made Jake jump up, keen-eyed and barking. Bob went to answer it, and Neil heard him order Jake to sit.

"Betty! Please come in," he was saying. "Of course I remember you."

Neil and Emily exchanged glances.

"That must be Betty Cooke," whispered Emily. "Milly's owner before Bev."

"No need to keep the taxi waiting, I'll take you home," said Bob. "Come and sit down."

He came in with an elderly white-haired woman, with a strong, rather stern face. She leaned a little on Bob's arm, and she spoke slowly, as if it was an effort to make her voice clear.

"I was so worried, when Bev came to me about Milly. On Firework Night, of all times for a dog to go missing! I rang her to see if there was any news, but there was no answer. Then I rang my taxi firm for someone to drive around

41

with me, looking for her. When I couldn't find her, I thought of coming here, in case somebody found her wandering and brought her in. But," she looked up with a worried frown, "she's not here, is she?"

"No, she isn't," said Bob gently. "She's at Mike Turner's surgery. There was an accident, Betty, but she should pull through." Simply and kindly, blaming no one, he told her what had happened. Neil and Emily saw the tension growing in her face.

"What was she thinking of?" demanded Betty. "How could she let poor Milly out on a night like this?"

"It wasn't Bev's fault," said Neil. "People were going in and out, doors got left open. Milly would have come straight back in, if the fireworks hadn't scared her."

"Fireworks, exactly!" insisted Betty, her speech becoming more slurred with agitation. "I've seen one of those posters up in her window, all about keeping your dogs indoors on Firework Night, but she couldn't even look after Milly!"

"I'm afraid accidents sometimes—" began Bob as Betty rose, stiffly but steadily.

"Accidents! Never mind accidents, this was

42

downright negligence! Doors don't leave themselves open, do they? I thought Milly had a good home, but Bev leaves her to go running about on the main road!"

Neil was burning to say that it wasn't like that, but he knew he'd only make matters worse. He clenched his fists tightly and didn't speak.

"I should like to go now," said Betty. "I understand you defending Bev. But there's no excuse for her carelessness."

She was still protesting as Bob helped her to the door to drive her home. "My poor little Milly!"

As the door shut behind them, Neil buried his hands in Jake's warm fur and fussed him.

"What are we going to do?" asked Emily.

"I don't suppose there's anything we can do," said Neil. For a moment, he stared into space. "I'm going to the office."

"What for?" asked Emily. "It's late already."

"I want to add to what I wrote about Milly on the website this morning. It's all out of date now, don't you see?"

Emily nodded. "Yes, I do."

"Milly deserves to be famous, and she will be. And everyone who reads about her will know what a good owner she has."

"I feel sorry for Betty," said Emily. "She's only angry because she loves Milly. She'll calm down."

"Do you think so?" said Neil. "I think she meant it. She's going to make trouble for Bev, and Bev's upset enough as it is."

"The main thing is that Milly's going to live," said Emily. "Mike seemed clear enough about that."

"That's not enough," said Neil. "She has to be herself again. Bright and clever, and happy. Nothing less." Even as he said it, he pictured her as he had last seen her, drugged and injured, sprawled helplessly on Mike's examination table. With that picture in his head, he went to the office, switched on the computer, and opened the website.

At the end of his piece about Milly as a King Street success story, he typed in the date.

It's Saturday night, he typed in. *Since I wrote that last piece, Milly . . .*

He stared at the screen and searched for the right words to write. Painfully, he lived through every moment of the evening again as he wrote his account of Milly's accident.

That's as much as I know, he typed at last. *I'll*

update this page when there's any news –
whatever it is.

Carole came in, and read it over his shoulder.

"You'll feel better now," she said. "Writing it all down and telling people will have helped."

"Maybe," said Neil. "But it doesn't matter how I feel. I just wish I could make everything right for Milly."

Chapter Five

It was still dark outside on Sunday when Neil sat up in his bed, wide awake. He switched on his bedside light. It had taken him ages to fall asleep. He'd tried counting sheep, but that had only made it worse. If he imagined sheep jumping over a gate they were being herded by a Border collie, and it was always the same one.

Every time, it was Sam, and when he thought of Sam he relived that terrible scene by the river. When he had finally fallen asleep his dreams had been confused and disturbing. Sometimes he dreamed that Sam was dying in his arms, then it was Milly, and then he was running to save a dog, knowing that he was running on the spot and couldn't get to it in time.

He rubbed his face and hunted for his watch. He may as well get up and take Jake for a walk.

He dressed quickly and went downstairs as quietly as he could. Jake was curled in his basket but he came readily to Neil, his eyes bright and his tail wagging, scampering to and fro as Neil reached for his lead. Neil took him to the exercise field where he could run wild, sniffing along the fence for all the new smells of the morning, pushing his nose into rabbit holes and mole hills, darting along scent trails. After the first burst of energy, Neil decided it was a good time for a bit of obedience practice before his dad's Sunday morning class.

"Stay!" Neil walked away, not looking over his shoulder, hoping all the time that Jake would stay put. When he did turn he saw Jake still on the spot, but standing, hopeful, anticipating the call.

"Stay!" Jake sat, his eyes still on Neil's face. When he was called he wandered up slowly, as if to tease Neil for keeping him waiting.

"Good boy! You took your time! Weren't you quite sure what I wanted?" Neil patted his left leg, and Jake walked round him to sit at his heel and gaze up at his face.

They tried the exercise again, but Neil knew
that little and often was the best way to train a
dog, so they soon turned for home. Jake was
shaping up well. One day, he could even be as
good as his father.

Walking down to the house, throwing a stick
for Jake, Neil thought about Milly again. He
wondered when they'd hear any news about
her, and whether she'd been able to sleep
comfortably during the night. Mike and Janice

would be kind to her, of course, but she must be missing Bev. It was all so hard to accept. A bit of confusion over a door, a firework, a couple of street lights that didn't work – and now Milly lay helplessly on a blanket, seriously injured.

A van was slowing to a halt outside the house, and Neil recognized it as Dan's builders' van. It had been a familiar sight at King Street when the new rescue centre had been under construction.

"Dan's here early," he said to Jake. "It's not time for obedience class yet."

Dan jumped down from the van and Neil quickly called to Jake, fastening on his lead in case Pooh-Bah made an appearance. Bob must have heard the engine too, because he came out of the house with a mug of tea in his hand. By the time Neil and Jake joined them Pooh-Bah was sniffing about on the ground, pulling at his lead as they approached. Jake and Pooh-Bah sniffed and circled at each other, while Neil struggled not to laugh. Pooh-Bah going round in circles looked like a mop on wheels – a mop that growled.

"Be quiet, Pooh-Bah," said Dan. "He won't harm your dog, Neil, so long as Jake doesn't come near me. He's very possessive."

"All Pekes are," said Neil.

"I know you saw that tussle with B-E-R-N-I-E," he said, "but he's not always like that."

"So you can't even say Be . . . that dog's name in front of him?" said Neil.

"That's why I came," said Dan. "What do you suggest, Bob? I've tried to keep the two of them apart, but this rascal keeps trying to dig under the fences to have a go at him."

Sarah ran out of the house, still finishing a mouthful of toast. She sat on the ground and cuddled both dogs at once.

"You may be trying too hard," said Bob. "They've got to learn to put up with each other. It would help if they could get used to meeting on neutral ground."

"What's newt – newtle – what you said?" asked Sarah.

"It means somewhere that doesn't belong to either of them," explained Bob. "So neither dog feels they have to defend it. We'll see if we can get John to bring Bernie to obedience class. It'll take time and patience, but we have to try. Neil, stop staring into space. Go and get your breakfast."

"I was thinking," said Neil. "There has to be a

reason. When dogs dig under fences, that's a sign of boredom, isn't it? Boredom or anxiety."

"Maybe he wants to get out of the garden," said Sarah, and rubbed her face against Pooh-Bah's head.

"It's worth thinking about," said Dan. "But I'll leave you folks to finish your breakfast. I want to take him for a run along the ridgeway before obedience class, but I'll leave the van here if that's OK with you."

Pooh-Bah trotted after Dan with a flurry of silky fur and the Parker family went into the house where Neil finally sat down to breakfast. He poured an enormous bowl of cornflakes, realizing suddenly how hungry he was.

"Pooh-Bah's a funny name," said Sarah. "It sounds rude."

"It's from an opera," said Carole, "*The Mikado*. Pooh-Bah was The Lord High Everything Else. He . . ."

She broke off as they heard footsteps in the hall. Bev appeared in the kitchen. All eating, drinking and conversation stopped. One look at her red-rimmed eyes and pale face showed that she had had a wretched night.

"I went to see her, first thing," she said, bravely fighting the unsteadiness in her voice.

"She's not in pain, but she's very groggy. Mike's not at all happy about that leg."

"Sit down, Bev," said Carole quickly, pushing a chair towards her and pouring a mug of tea.

"He's going to do X-rays this morning," Bev went on. "Poor thing, she looked at me, and she just couldn't understand why I couldn't make her better. I'd give anything to turn the clock back. Bob, do you want any help with obedience class?"

"There's no need . . ." began Bob, but Bev didn't let him finish.

"There is," she said. "I need to keep busy today."

Later that morning, Neil took Jake to obedience class as planned, but it was hard to concentrate.

"You're very quiet today, Neil," said Bob as they walked back to the house afterwards. "It's Milly, isn't it?"

Neil nodded miserably. "That's the worst thing, with dogs," he said. "They don't understand what's happening. Suddenly they're in pain and in a strange place, and you can't explain it to them."

"It's hard," agreed Bob. "All you can do is be

there, and be kind, and hope it helps. And it does."

"Maybe it does," said Neil, "but it isn't enough. Milly's never going to be the same again."

Everyone, even Sarah, was subdued for the whole of that day, and at breakfast the next morning there was tension in the air. Nobody had much to say. The school day dragged to an end at last and Neil, coming home, saw Bev bringing three of the rescue dogs back from their walk. He hurried to join her, helping her to put the happily panting dogs back in their pens and fill their water dishes. He could see she was doing her best to carry on as usual, though her mind was obviously with Milly. When a car door banged she jumped, and went straight to the door.

"It's Mike," she said. "He's going into the office."

"You go, Bev," said Neil. "I'll finish off here."

It didn't take him long, and five minutes later he headed towards the office to see what was happening. He arrived in time to see Kate gently leading a tearful Bev from the room, and Mike's face was grave.

"There's no easy way to say things like this,

Neil," he said, "and it's not as bad as it sounds. But I've just had to tell Bev there's no way I can save Milly's leg. I'm going to have to amputate."

"Oh, but . . ." The news seemed so hard and so final that Neil fought against it. "There must be something you can do!"

"If there was, Neil, I'd do it," said Mike. "Even in a younger dog, there'd be little chance of the leg mending, but Milly's not young any more. It has to be done."

"It's so unfair!" Neil burst out. "Milly's so – so alive, and so bright. She's enjoyed life so much until now."

"I know," said Mike, "and she will again. But she'll get better much quicker without that damaged leg and I don't think we should wait. I'm going to operate straight away, so as soon as Bev's finished here, I'll drive her to the surgery."

"She can go now," said Carole. "The sooner it's done, the better. I'll go and have a word with her. I just wish I could be more help."

Carole brought Bev back in. Her face was swollen with tears as she picked up her coat and her bag.

"I don't know what I'm doing here anyway," she said. She glanced up at the office pin board, covered with photographs of King Street's success stories and doggy friends – Dotty and her puppies, Max and Prince, Red, Sam, Bramble, Mrs Lumley's dogs.

"I don't belong here," she said. "I shouldn't keep a dog. I'm not a fit person to be anywhere near them. Especially one like Milly."

"But Bev . . ." began Neil. But she was already striding purposefully out of the office after Mike.

Chapter Six

Neil ran after Bev. It might not be the best time to say it, but he couldn't help himself.

"Bev," he said, "if you shouldn't keep a dog, neither should I. You've heard about that day when Jake escaped, haven't you? He was tiny, he'd only just come here and there was thick snow on the ground. Somehow the back door was open, and he got out! He was shivering and exhausted when I found him. He could have died of exposure, and it would have been my fault! We all make mistakes."

He wasn't sure if Bev was listening. Desperately, he tried to think of some way to help. "I'll come with you to Mike's if you like."

"Thanks, Neil." She tried to smile, but couldn't quite manage it. "It'll be good to have you there."

"I'll just let Mum know where I'll be," he said.

Carole was still in the office, where Emily was using the computer. She nodded silently when Neil told her what he planned to do.

"Bev needs all the support she can get," she said. "She's looking after Milly, and we're going to look after her."

"Give her my love," said Emily, glancing up from the screen. "I've got a homework project to do, but I'll be thinking about Milly."

"And, Neil," said Carole, "if Mike says Milly can go straight home after the op, phone me. One of us will come and give Bev and Milly a lift home."

"Do you think that will happen?" Neil was surprised. "Will Milly be able to go home today?"

"If the operation goes smoothly, she'll only need TLC, and Bev's the best person to give her that. If Bev wants to bring her in to work while she's recovering, that's fine too. We'll find her a pen."

Neil smiled and then left.

*

Lying on Mike's operating table, Milly looked peaceful. Her tongue lolled out of her mouth. Bev held her head, talking softly to her.

"She's completely under the anaesthetic now," said Mike. "She can't hear you any more." He wore his green gown, and was pulling on rubber gloves. Neil noticed the tray of sharp instruments behind him, and hoped that Bev hadn't seen it.

"If you go through to the waiting room, I'll call you both as soon as it's over," said Mike. "Janice will be assisting me during the operation."

Neil took a last look at Milly and went out with Bev to the waiting room, as Mike was fastening a surgical mask over his nose and mouth.

They sat in silence on the green padded seats and waited. Neil had soon read all the posters about vaccinations, flea treatments, worming tablets and not leaving dogs in hot cars. For the twentieth time, Bev looked at her watch.

"It feels as if we've been sitting here for ever," she said. "Neil, are you sure it's all right to bring Milly to the kennels after this?"

"It's the best place for her! We can find her a pen, or she can just curl up in the kitchen."

"That might be good," admitted Bev.

"Jake would like it," said Neil. "He'd have company again."

But the mention of Jake made Bev think again. "On second thoughts, no," she said. "He might pester her. Do you think I could keep her in the office? That would be quiet, but there's always somebody popping in and out. You could nip in and see her, couldn't you Neil, after school?"

"Try and stop me!"

"The thing is," she said, with a nervous glance at the surgery door, "I don't want to let her out of my sight. I'm the one she trusts, and it's my fault this has happened. I have to be there for her."

"But we're all . . ." began Neil, and stopped as the door opened. Immediately, Bev was on her feet. Mike took off his mask and gave them a reassuring smile.

"All done now," he said. "She's still very sleepy, but she'll start to come round soon. Now it's over, she'll be fine."

"Fine?" exclaimed Bev. "Missing a hind leg?"

"Believe me," said Mike, "she's not the first dog to go through this and she won't be the last. They generally come through it fighting fit.

Especially a dog like Milly, in excellent condition with a tremendous spirit – you just wait and see."

"Even at her age?" queried Bev.

"She's not young, but she's not ancient either," Mike reassured her. "And she's not overweight, so she hasn't too much body weight to manage on three legs. I'm sure she won't let this hold her back. She can even go home straight away. Come and see her."

Milly was lying on her side. Where her left hind leg had been, there was a neatly bandaged stump. Neil saw Bev bite her lip hard.

"Oh, Milly!" she said softly. At the sound of her voice, Milly half opened her eyes. She tried to raise her head but sank back, and her eyes closed again.

"Brave girl, Milly!" said Neil.

"That's right, she needs to hear your voices," said Mike. "She can't respond much, but she can probably hear you."

"How will she ever walk properly again?" said Bev. "How can she balance?"

"She'll sort that one out for herself," said Mike. "Small dogs recover from this operation better than bigger ones. They're lighter, so they put less strain on the other limbs. In a few days she'll come back and get her stitches out – Janice will give you an appointment. After that, she'll be running about like a greyhound."

Neil could see from Bev's face that she didn't believe him. Mike was usually right, though.

"You'll see," went on Mike. "I did this same operation for a little spaniel bitch a while back. There's no stopping her now."

Neil stroked Milly's head, and her eyes flickered open. At least she seemed to know she was safe, and being cared for.

"Is there anything I have to do?" asked Bev. "Any special care, until she has the stitches out?"

"Just keep the dressing clean and dry," said Mike. "If you're worried, bring her back. I'll change the dressing if necessary. You're perfectly capable of doing it yourself, but I'll do it here if you're worried. And I'll give her a special collar. Neil, can you get one, please? They're in the cupboard on your right."

Neil found the funnel-shaped plastic collars and Mike fastened one gently around Milly's neck. It completely hid her head, and Bev knelt down at the end of the table so that the dog could still see her.

"It's a nuisance, I know," said Mike. "But it'll

stop her from tearing the dressing with her teeth. As soon as she wants to get up and about, let her. She'll know if she's well enough."

To Neil, Milly looked as if she'd never walk again – but he knew Mike could be trusted. He went to the reception desk to phone home. Emily answered.

"How is she?" his sister asked anxiously.

"She looks awful, but Mike says she'll be all right. Can you get Mum or Dad to pick us up?"

Carole was well equipped when she arrived in the Range Rover. She had brought a pet carrier, a blanket, and a handmade card from Sarah with a picture of Milly on the front and Get Well Soon inside, with kisses.

"Come on, then, Miss Milly," said Carole. "Do you want her in the carrier, Bev?"

"No, I'll carry her." Bev wrapped Milly in the blanket, cradling her as she carried her out.

All the way home her face was white and strained. Neil talked to Milly, telling her how brave she was, knowing that it didn't much matter what he said, so long as he said it kindly. Once, Milly strained her head round in an attempt to see what had happened to the leg, but the effort was enormous and she lay down again, too weak to care. Outside Bev's house,

Carole glided the Range Rover to a halt.

"I'll take Milly while you get out, Bev," she said.

"No, I'll manage." Bev held Milly firmly. "It's better if she stays with me. Fish in my pocket for the keys, Neil, and open the door. If the cat's there, don't let her near Milly."

"You've got company," said Carole, and Neil heard the uncertainty in her voice. He looked round to see Betty Cooke, leaning on her stick, walking towards them in her slow, lopsided way.

"I thought I should come and see how Milly

is," she said, very slowly and deliberately. Neil wondered if she felt hurt at being left out of things.

"She's doing really well," he said. "Mike's pleased with her." But Betty was bending over the limp bundle in Bev's arms.

"Doing well?" she peered in horror. "Why does she have to wear that collar – has she . . .?" The blanket had slipped a little – only a little, but it was enough. "Oh, Milly! She hasn't lost the leg, has she? My poor Milly!"

"It had to be done," said Carole gently. "And Bev is taking excellent care of her."

"It's a pity, Bev, you couldn't take care of her on Saturday night," said Betty. Neil thought she sounded like a sarcastic teacher. He said something about it not being Bev's fault, but that only made it worse.

"Well, it's hardly Milly's fault, is it, that she ran onto the road? I should have kept her."

Neil decided that this wasn't the best time to point out that she couldn't possibly have kept her. "Milly should be indoors," he said, "where it's warm."

"Yes, unlock the door, Neil, and Milly can get to her own bed," said Carole, and added firmly, "and I'll drive you home, Betty."

Neil let them into the house, scooping up the cat under one arm. Milly's empty basket lay near the hearth and with great care, Bev laid Milly down.

Neil could see that there wasn't much he could do for Milly just now. In the kitchen, he set about making tea while Steppy clawed at the door.

"Sorry, Steppy, but Bev says no," he said. "You won't be popular if you go bothering Milly." But he knew it was pointless. Steppy, like all cats, would do exactly as she wanted. As soon as Neil carried in the tray, she squeezed past and ran to Milly.

"Steppy! No!" Bev pushed the cat aside. "Milly can't play with you now."

"Watch, and see what she does," said Neil. "We won't let her do any harm."

The cat sniffed delicately at Milly's nose and Milly, opening her eyes, sniffed back. Steppy seemed suspicious of the bandaged leg, sniffing from a distance and backing away.

"She doesn't like the smell of disinfectant, I suppose," said Neil. "She won't bother Milly."

Milly struggled to stand, but Bev reached out to settle her down again.

"Leave her," advised Neil. "Mike says she'll

know what she can do and what she can't."

"That's easy for you to say," said Bev sharply. "She isn't your dog, or Mike's, either."

Together they watched, Neil with keen interest and Bev with lip-biting anxiety. Milly, with a determined effort, rolled onto her front paws and dragged herself up onto Bev's lap. With a deep sigh she laid down her head, closed her eyes again, and settled down to sleep. The doorbell rang, but Milly ignored it.

"Well done, Milly!" said Neil. "She knew she needed her mum. And here's my mum back." He opened the door for Carole, who came to sit on the floor beside them.

"That's right, Milly, you sleep it off," said Carole. "It's the anaesthetic, not the operation, that's making her feel rough."

"What did Betty say to you?" asked Bev.

"Never mind Betty," said Carole. "She's upset."

"She blames me for Milly's accident, and she's right." Bev felt in her sleeve for a tissue. "If only I'd remembered the sedative. If only . . ."

Neil knew all about "if only". He knew how Bev felt. If only he hadn't taken Sam and Jake out that day. If only they'd gone a longer way round, instead of crossing the bridge.

"It's no good, Bev," he said. "When Sam died, I blamed myself. But it happened, like Milly's accident, and you can't change things." He stroked Milly's ears. "You have to go on."

"And dogs will be dogs," said Carole. "Sam was a Border collie. They belong outdoors, on the hills. When we knew he was ill we could have kept him at home and coddled him like a pet lamb, but he would have hated it. You can't keep Milly in a plastic bubble, Bev. She'd be unhappy if you treated her like an ornament."

When Andrew arrived home from work, Neil and Carole decided it was time to go.

"Neil," said Bev, "There's a letter on the hall table. Will you post it on your way home?"

Neil picked it up. It was addressed to The Secretary, Compton Open Dog Show, 25 Elmtree Gardens, Compton.

"When I got home last night, I wrote to withdraw her from the show," said Bev. "She obviously can't take part now."

"Mike said she'd be fine after the stitches come out," said Neil, slipping the envelope into his pocket.

"No," said Bev firmly. "She's not going to an obedience event. Certainly not this month, and probably never again."

Neil knew it was no use to argue, but when he reached home he went straight to the office. Emily was just finishing her project.

"Don't shut down the computer," he said. "I need to update Milly's story."

There's more news of Milly, he typed in. *As our vet, Mike, said, it isn't easy to tell.*

It certainly wasn't, and it took a lot of false starts before he had completed writing up the news of Milly. Finally, he wrote:

. . . so Milly will never be the same again, but she's a fighter and she'll do her best to live a normal life. If ever a dog deserves to win through, Milly does.

Chapter Seven

"**N**eil! Come and get your breakfast before I feed it to Jake!"

"In a minute!" called Neil. He hurried into the kitchen, both arms full of an untidy sheaf of papers.

Emily poured him a mug of tea. "What's all this?" she said, picking up the loose pages he had just dumped on the kitchen table.

"E-mails! Dozens of them, about Milly! Look at this! It's taken ages to print them all out! Just read them!" He had gone down to the office early to check out the website before breakfast.

Emily flicked through them. "They're from all over the place!"

Some of the messages were brief and kind –

very best wishes to Milly, and *I hope Milly's chasing rabbits again soon.* Some were full of sympathy, but the most encouraging ones were from other owners whose dogs had lost a leg, all describing how well they had recovered.

There was one that Neil particularly liked. "Listen to this one. *I have a seven-year-old King Charles spaniel bitch, Mara, who had a similar accident nearly a year ago. I want you to know that she gets around as well on three legs as she did on four. She's always been a great one for jumping and running in and out of things and seems to think she's an acrobat. I'd love to meet Milly when she's back to normal, and I'm sure that won't be long.*"

"That's so encouraging," said Emily.

"Isn't it! His name's Will Hammick, and he's given his home address," said Neil. "It's near Padsham."

"That's a must, then," said Emily.

Neil glanced at the clock and hastily took a gulp of tea. Carole came to look at the e-mails.

"There's a lot of interest in Milly," she remarked. "I wonder if the local press would take it up?"

"Great idea!" Neil left the table and was soon through to the switchboard of the local

70

newspaper, the *Compton News*.

"Hello, can I speak to Jake Fielding, please?" he asked. Jake, the young staff photographer, had covered dog stories for them in the past. Neil explained the situation quickly.

"Milly will be here this afternoon, Jake," he said. "Do you want to come and get a picture?" Jake was very keen, and arranged to come over later that day, when Neil was back from school.

He was just finishing when Bev arrived for work.

"Where's Milly?" Sarah, who had been trying to wriggle into her shoes without unfastening them first, jumped up.

"How's Milly?" asked Neil. "Get down, Jake, leave Bev alone."

"She's in her basket in the car," said Bev. "I didn't want to bring her in here in case Jake frightened her. I'll put her in the office."

"I'll do it!" Neil gulped down the rest of his tea, and got down from the table.

"No, I'll do it myself, thanks," said Bev. "Shouldn't you finish your breakfast before school?"

Neil ate quickly, then went out to the car. Emily was already there.

Milly was sitting up in her basket with her

71

head up, her ears lifted in the funnel collar and her eyes on the house. At the sight of Neil and Emily she let out a few subdued barks and as they came nearer, they could see the wagging of her tail.

"Wow!" said Neil. "Last time I saw her, she was sleeping off the anaesthetic."

"Well, she's certainly slept it off now," said Emily. "She looks pretty good."

"She's a different dog from yesterday," said Neil. "She's sitting lopsided, to keep the weight off her left side, but she looks comfortable."

Milly was straining to see past them with eager dark eyes, then she barked again. They looked over their shoulders as Bev and Bob came from the house. Bob had a letter in his hand. "Think about it, Bev," he was saying. "This isn't the right time to make decisions."

Jake gave Neil a lick, then ran round the car for a good sniff.

"It's kind of you, Bob, but I have to resign," said Bev. "I'll work a month's notice, and go. After what's happened, I shouldn't be looking after animals. Betty's right."

"What? You can't go!" insisted Neil.

Emily seemed equally shocked. "We can't manage without you!"

"If I ever needed to leave Jake with someone," insisted Neil, "I'd trust you with him."

"That's very kind of you, Neil," she said, "but you can't expect all the King Street clients to think the same. I'm a bad advert for this place."

"Aren't you going to get her out of the car?" asked Emily. Milly was whining with her head on one side, wondering why Bev was keeping her waiting.

"Um – yes," said Bev, but Neil could see she was uneasy. "Neil, call Jake and hang on to him in case he jumps up at her. Bob, will you carry her basket?"

"Don't you want to let her try a few steps on her own?" said Bob.

Bev cradled Milly closely in her arms, but Milly sniffed eagerly at Neil and Emily. She wanted to be down. "No, not here," she said quickly. "She managed a few steps in the garden this morning."

"Well done, Milly," said Neil, grinning as he tickled her under her chin.

". . . but I don't want to put her on the ground," Bev went on. "Other dogs have been here, and I don't want her to catch any infections."

Neil and Emily exchanged glances. Bev was

being extremely cautious with Milly.

"What's she likely to catch?" asked Neil.

"Nothing to what you two will catch if you don't get off to school," said Bob. "Scarper!"

"Dad," called Neil as he wheeled out his bike, "show Bev those e-mails!"

Gossip travelled quickly in Compton. At Meadowbank School, everyone was asking about Milly. Neil had to answer the same questions all day – is she all right? Is it true that she's going to die? Has she really lost both hind legs? Will she have to be put to sleep? By the end of the afternoon he felt he'd turned into an answering machine, and he hurried to get home. He wanted to be there in time for Milly's photo opportunity.

"Is Jake here yet?" he called as he ran into the house. The young dog bounded up to him, and Neil ruffled his ears. "Not you, stupid! Mum, is Jake Fielding here?"

"He's on the way up to the exercise field, with Bev," said Carole.

Neil zoomed outside. At the exercise field he caught up with Jake Fielding, who as usual had his hair in a pony tail and his pockets stuffed with spare films. Bev was with him, holding

Milly in her arms and stroking her head as Jake loaded up a new film.

"It will look a lot better if you put her down," Jake was saying. Bev didn't look too sure, but Milly wriggled in her arms when she saw Neil.

"She mustn't get the dressing wet," explained Bev. "She could get cross-infections."

Neil remembered the events earlier that morning. Bev wouldn't put Milly down then, either.

"There's a patch of bare, clean earth here," he suggested. "And she can sit on my jacket. She really wants to be down, don't you, Milly?"

"I suppose . . ." said Bev, though she still didn't sound happy about it. "I don't really know what good this is going to do, Neil. I'm not sure I want Milly in the papers and everybody knowing about my carelessness."

Neil tried to make her see sense. "This is about *Milly*, Bev. She's an inspiration because she has been so brave despite all of her suffering. Her story will help loads of other people realize that losing a limb is not the end of the world."

The photographer nodded as he changed the lens on his camera. "That's right, Bev."

Bev sighed. "OK." With great care she put

Milly down and knelt on the ground beside her. "I suppose that is a worthwhile reason . . ." Milly, stiff and sore as she was, hobbled slowly in a circle. She moved cautiously, but she stayed upright.

"Well done, girl," said Neil, and gave her a dog treat.

"That's the most she's done yet," said Bev. "She mustn't do too much, and wear herself out."

"Can you come in a bit closer, Bev?" asked Jake, crouching down as he focused the camera. "Neil, we'll have you in this too." The shutter clicked repeatedly. "Stay there. Let's just have one more."

"Only one," said Bev. "It's less than twenty-four hours since her operation, she's still quite poorly."

Neil leaned over to look at Milly's face inside the plastic collar. She craned her neck and tried to lick him.

"Did you see the e-mails that have come in in response to the feature on our website?" he asked.

"Yes, Carole told me," said Bev. "I think there have been more today, too. One of the national doggy magazines has picked up Milly's story.

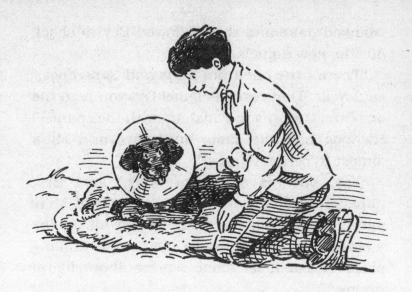

They said they hope you'll keep updating the details on the website."

"Cool!" said Neil. "Which magazine?"

"*Dogs and Superdogs*, I think." Bev was more concerned with inspecting Milly's dressing, but Neil was ecstatic.

"The best! Milly, you'll be a star! You'll be the most photographed dog in the country."

She might be, he thought, and every single picture will show Bev clinging on to her. He knew Bev wasn't usually like this.

"Right, that'll do," said Jake.

Bev scooped Milly up in her arms and carried her back to her basket in the office. Neil thanked Jake and then followed Bev to check out the new e-mails.

"There's the one from *Dogs and Superdogs*," said Neil. "That really is fame! Did you read the one from that guy in Padsham with the spaniel? His dog had the same operation, and she's almost hyperactive now!"

"Yes, but his dog's not Milly," said Bev, impatiently. "No two dogs are alike, and Milly may not adapt in the same way at all. At the moment, I can't imagine her even walking properly again, let alone tearing about like a puppy."

Give her a chance, thought Neil. *You're not helping her.* But it was no use trying to say so. Bev wouldn't accept it just now.

"It's time I went home," said Bev. "I think I'll call at Mike's on the way, and ask him to check her dressing. And he hasn't said a word about the bill. I'd better mention it."

"Can I come with you?" said Neil. He wanted to be with Milly, even though Bev would barely let anyone touch her.

As Bev picked her up again Milly's eyes searched the ground and her ears were sharply pricked, as if she couldn't wait to be down again, sniffing and exploring. She wagged her tail hopefully as Bob came in.

"Can I go now, Bob?" said Bev. "I'll just need to get my coat. I left it in the kitchen."

"Yes – um . . ." Bob didn't often looked awkward, but he did now. "Take Milly to the car. Neil will bring your coat."

Bev was happy to take Milly and put her in the car, but Neil wondered what was going on. Why didn't his father want her in the kitchen?

He soon found out. He heard voices as he went to fetch the coat. Seated in the kitchen with his mother was Betty Cooke.

"The point is that I trusted you to find someone who would take good care of my dog," she was saying.

"I think you'll agree, Betty," said Carole, with great patience, "that there have been no problems until now. Bev's brought Milly to see you every week, hasn't she? You've seen for yourself that Milly's always been happy and healthy. Bev is a good owner, and she hasn't turned into a bad one just because of an accident that was beyond her control."

"You don't understand," said Betty with rising exasperation. "Bev isn't . . . isn't . . . oh, it's no good trying to explain. Please telephone for my taxi."

Neil had heard enough. He grabbed Bev's coat and went out to the car.

Milly cowered and growled softly when they reached the surgery. She had no pleasant memories of this place, however kind Mike and Janice were. She lay submissively as Mike inspected the dressing, but Neil could see her eyes were wide with fear. He crouched at the end of the table, his face close to hers, stroking her head, whispering reassurance to her.

"I was afraid she might have got it dirty," said Bev. "She might have wet it, or picked up something from the ground."

"Nothing at all to worry about," said Mike. "You can't stop a dog being a dog."

"Yes," said Bev, reaching inside the collar to scratch Milly's head. "But this is *my* dog."

Milly scrabbled to sit up, tried to look at her injury, and found she couldn't see past the collar. She twisted as she tried to inspect the dressing, and flopped down again.

"She wants to know what's going on," said Mike. "She's doing fine. Bring her on Saturday to have the stitches out."

Walking home, Neil was still wondering about those words, "my dog". Betty had called

Milly that too. He tried to imagine what it would be like if he ever had to part with Jake. If something terrible happened, if he had to hand Jake over to somebody else, would he ever really feel that he'd given him away? Perhaps he could understand how Betty felt about Milly, and why she was so upset.

When he got home he found Bev's letter to the secretary of the dog show, still in his pocket. He'd forgotten all about it, but tomorrow would do. There was still over a week before the show. Just now, there was the website to update.

It wasn't just *Dogs and Superdogs* magazine that wanted to know about Milly. There were the dozens of well-wishers who cared about her, too. It seemed as if the whole country wanted her to get well.

He couldn't very well tell them that Milly's newest problem was an over-protective owner. He sat down and began to type:

Today, Milly looks one hundred per cent better than she did. She even took a few steps on her own . . .

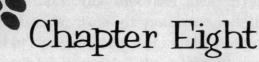

Chapter Eight

Saturday morning brought another flood of e-mails. Will Hammick, Mara's owner, was becoming a regular correspondent. Sean Appleby, the unfortunate driver of the car that had injured Milly, had sent his good wishes, too. Neil was typing in a further diary entry when Emily came in followed by Jake, carrying a ball.

"In a minute, Jake." Neil leaned over to scratch Jake's head. "Just let me reply to this lot. Em, how do you spell 'recuperating'?"

"Just say she's getting better," said Emily. "She is, isn't she?"

"She is, but she'd do it faster if Bev would just put her down now and again and let her look after herself. Em, will you finish this? I'll take Jake out for a run, then I'm going to Mike's. Milly's stitches are coming out today."

Emily smiled. "Give her a hug from me!"

Neil met Bev and Milly back at Mike's surgery after his morning clinic at King Street. It was all very well for Emily to say "give Milly a hug", but she'd be a lot more huggable without the plastic collar. They soothed the anxious dog as Mike gently unwound the bandages and snipped the stitches.

"That's healed beautifully!" he said. "Well done, Milly!"

Milly, hearing her name, sat up. She was doing that easily now, Neil noticed.

"She shouldn't need that collar anymore," Mike added, as Milly twisted her neck and tried to inspect the stump of her leg. "I don't think she'll do herself any harm from now on."

"May I keep it for a few days more, all the same?" asked Bev. "In case she does try to chew the leg – I mean, the wound." She picked Milly up and tucked her under one arm.

"She can walk," smiled Mike. "The more, the better. Her muscles will get lazy if she doesn't use them."

"I'll carry her to reception, all the same," said Bev. Neil stayed behind.

"I'm worried about Milly," he said quietly to Mike. "You've seen what Bev's like."

"I know. She's still blaming herself for the accident, so she's making up for it by never letting her take chances. It's a problem, Neil, but I don't think Bev can help it. Anyway, let me know how they're doing. Ask Janice to send in the next patient, please."

Bev was talking to Janice at the desk, and Neil saw Dan and Pooh-Bah in the waiting room. He knelt to pat Pooh-Bah, and the little dog wagged his tail excitedly. Then he sneezed, and his whole coat rippled.

"Bless you!" laughed Neil. He patted Pooh-Bah and ruffled the fur around his collar. However glamorous Pooh-Bah looked, he was a real dog at heart, just like Jake and Milly. Neil looked closely at his eyes.

"His eyes look watery today," he said. "Is he all right?"

"I think he's just got a bit of grit in them from digging under the fence. I've brought him here to check there's no damage."

"Pekes do get problems with grit," said Neil. "All dogs with prominent eyes do. If you must dig, Pooh-Bah, what do you expect?"

"I've tried nailing boards to the bottom of the fence," said Dan. "He can't get under, but it doesn't stop him trying."

"I have to go, Bev's waiting," said Neil. "We'll see you at training class tomorrow, won't we?"

"I asked about Mike's fee," Bev said on the way home. "He says it's all been paid by Sean Appleby."

"Sean Appleby? The driver who . . . er . . ."

"Knocked her down, yes."

"He's been leaving messages on the website, asking about her," said Neil. "And so has Will Hammick, the man with the spaniel who lost a leg. He'd love to meet Milly."

"We're home," said Bev briskly, changing the subject. She parked the car on her drive, and Neil reached for Milly's lead. "You won't need that, Neil, I'll carry her to the door."

"Mike says she has to walk!" said Neil. "Her muscles will weaken."

Bev gave a little sigh and a frown. "I suppose so. But make sure her lead is on before you open the car door."

Neil understood Bev's anxiety and slipped on the lead. They were very near to the spot where

Milly had been knocked down. He took off the plastic collar, as she was hardly going to chew at her stump while there were more interesting things to do, like sniffing round the garden. As soon as the door was opened, Milly sprang down from the car.

She staggered on landing and wobbled as she hopped from one front paw to the other. But she didn't fall, and she limped along beside Neil with determination. In the garden she hobbled from one plant to the next, sniffing with great interest, eager and inquisitive as ever. Free from bandages and the irritating collar, she almost looked like her old self.

"I'll just check where the cat is," said Bev. She disappeared into the house, but soon came back to the door. "I've shut Steppy in the kitchen. You'll have to lift Milly over the doorstep."

"Lift you?" said Neil to Milly. "Does she think I'm going to lift you? You show us what you can do!"

Milly put two paws on the step. Then she stopped, head on one side, working out what to do next.

"No, Neil!" said Bev. "She can't possibly manage that!" And before Milly could make the attempt, Bev was carrying her into the house. Neil followed.

"I'll get her a drink," he said.

"No, I will." Bev settled Milly in her basket. "Just watch her, please."

Milly, investigating her basket, found her teddy bear and dropped it at Neil's feet.

"Come on, then!" grinned Neil, and threw it a little way.

"NO!" Before Milly could retrieve the toy, Bev had pounced on it and given it to her. "Neil, will you stop interfering! Just because you come from King Street, you needn't think you can take over my dog!"

"Sorry," said Neil. Perhaps he had overstepped the mark, but he was only thinking of Milly. "I'd better go."

"I think that might be best," said Bev firmly. But when Neil opened the door, he found somebody else arriving.

"It's you!" he said. "You left e-mails for Milly! You're . . ."

"The villain who knocked Milly over in the first place, yes." He extended a hand to Neil and smiled at Bev, standing in the hall with Milly in her arms. "Sean Appleby. And I remember you, Neil. I came to see how Milly's doing. Your website diary is really good. I've been gripped. I'm sure a lot of other people have been too."

From his coat pocket he took a yellow plastic bone that jangled as he held it up. Milly wagged her tail in excitement, pricked her ears and tipped her head to one side.

"May I give her a present, Bev? How's she doing?"

He put the toy on the floor, and Bev set Milly down. Milly pounced on the bone, shook it, and gave it to Neil to throw. He glanced uncertainly at Bev.

"Just a little throw, Neil," she said. Milly fell

as she jumped at it, but she found her balance again.

Neil took advantage of the distraction of a new visitor and chanced his luck. "Bev, I was hoping to take her for a walk. Just a very little one. I'll keep her on the lead."

"I need to walk my dog, too," said Sean. "But he needs a lot of exercise."

Neil sat up in delight. "You've got a dog?"

"Yes, his name's Fergus. He's a what's-its-name, a wolf thing. You can meet him, if you like. He could do with a walk, but he might be a bit boisterous for Milly."

"Definitely," said Bev firmly. Neil wondered what a "wolf thing" was, and if Fergus was a Husky. There was a mew and a scratch at the kitchen door and Milly hopped across to it, pressing her nose to the tiny gap at floor level.

"And now she wants Steppy," sighed Bev. "All right, Neil, but keep her on a short lead. Just five minutes, mind."

Neil had looked forward to Milly's first walk. She limped bravely round the park, glancing up at him. She was struggling, but she was enjoying it, too, sniffing the scents on the fresh air. Other dog owners noticed her, and Neil wondered if they had followed the website diary or seen her picture in the newspaper. The five minutes were soon up, and he turned for home.

Walking back to Bev's, he noticed Sean's grey Rover with a dog grille in the back. He decided not to anger Fergus by approaching with another dog, but he was longing to meet the "wolf thing".

"She's exhausted!" cried Bev, as Milly limped into the house.

Milly lapped some water noisily, then scratched at the blanket in her basket – but this proved to be a wobbly business and Bev reached out to smooth the blanket.

"There, Milly. That'll be comfortable," she said.

"That's not how she likes it," smiled Neil. "Look!" Milly didn't want a neat blanket. She took it firmly in her teeth, gave it a good shaking and, having settled it the way she wanted it, put herself to bed. Neil stroked her head and she gave a glance of triumph before curling up for a sleep.

"Come and meet Fergus, Neil," said Sean. "We'll take him round the park."

Neil jumped to his feet. "See you on Monday, Bev," he said.

"So will I," said Sean. "I have some freebies for Milly. Do you use Pro-Pet dog foods?"

"Yes, they're very good," said Bev.

Neil knew they used Pro-Pet sometimes at King Street, too.

"I'm in advertising, and I handle their contract," said Sean, smiling. "Let's go, Neil. We'll let Fergus out."

The click of Sean's key in the lock woke the sleeping dog. From behind the dog grille rose a great craggy grey head, then two enormous paws.

"He's no beauty, but he's a great dog," said Sean. Fergus unfolded himself revealing legs longer than Neil would have thought possible. He slithered from the car, shaking himself with a flurry of grey hairs. In one easy movement, he put his paws on Sean's chest and wagged his tail.

"An Irish wolfhound! He's magnificent!" gasped Neil. "Fergus!" The dog, alert and full of energy, bounded over to him. Standing, his head came nearly to Neil's shoulder. He sniffed Neil thoroughly, wagged his tail, sat, and offered a paw.

"He's very gentle, in spite of the look of him," Sean said. "He's a kitten. But he's a good guard

dog. I can leave him in the car with all the windows open in summer, and know that nobody's going to touch it." He hunted in the back of the car, and emerged with a poop scoop and some plastic bags. "Come on, then, Fergus, come and tire yourself out."

"That can't be easy," grinned Neil on the way into the park.

"He's brilliant, but he does take a lot of exercise," agreed Sean, giving Neil the lead. "Luckily, we live in the country. Round here there seem to be fewer places now that you can take dogs. Even in the parks they have to be kept on leads."

"That's because of children playing," said Neil. "Not all people are as careful as you about poop-scoops. And uncontrolled dogs can be dangerous."

"Why can't they have a fenced-off area?" said Sean. "With a high fence, so athletes like Fergus can't jump over it and a spring on the gate so it can't be left open. Has nobody thought of that?"

"If they have, they haven't done anything about it," said Neil. He contracted the lead a little to pull Fergus away from a dead bird.

"Oh, why can't places be more dog-friendly?" said Sean with impatience. "I'd like to see poster campaigns about good dog-handling."

"We've just done one!" said Neil, and told Sean all about the posters he and Emily had been giving out before Bonfire Night. By the time he'd finished they were back at the car, and Sean drove him home.

"I'll keep in touch," said Sean. "Keep checking your e-mail! You're doing a great job for Milly."

Neil went straight to the computer to write up his account of Milly's first walk. He was finishing when Emily came in.

"How is she?" she asked.

"Which one?" replied Neil. "Milly's great. Bev's worse than ever."

"Will Hammick phoned," said Emily. "He wants us to take Milly there on Monday, after school, to meet Mara."

"It could be a breakthrough for Bev," said Neil. "If she sees Mara, she'll see everything that Milly could be, given the chance. But she'll probably refuse to go."

"Somebody's got to do something," said Emily, "to make sure we get Bev, Milly and Mara in the same place. And I think somebody has to be . . ."

"Us?" grinned Neil.

"Right!" said Emily.

Chapter Nine

"Lovely day for training class!" grumbled Bob in the barn on Sunday morning. It was an overcast day, with a cold wind gusting from the north, and the dogs and owners for obedience class would soon be arriving. "I'll have a barn full of hyperactive dogs. Rough weather always makes them excitable."

"Jake's daft!" giggled Sarah. Jake, much to her amusement, was chasing his tail, catching it and falling over.

"And we've got the Battle of Park Street Fence this morning," Bob went on. "Pooh-Bah and Bernie are coming."

"You told Dan and John to bring them, Dad?

Pooh-Bah and Bernie together?" said Emily.

"I should have hired a UN peace-keeping force," muttered Bob, but at this point dogs and owners began to arrive.

The barn was soon full of dogs, some sniffing the ground, some sitting up watchfully, some making threatening noises and others dozing through it all. One of the dozy ones was Bernie, who lay with his heavy head on his paws and his eyes half open. Next to John Cartwright and Bernie sat Toby Sparrow, with Scrap at his feet.

"Hi, Toby! Hi, Scrap!" Neil and Emily went straight to their friend, and were welcomed with enthusiastic jumping from the little Dalmatian. "How's he doing, Toby?"

"He's great. And he can do his obedience training properly if he wants to," said Toby, who wouldn't have cared if Scrap was the naughtiest dog in England. "But he can't stay still for long."

Just then, Bernie raised his head from his paws. A growl rose in his throat, getting louder. Neil didn't need to look round to see who had just arrived.

"Easy, Bernie. Quiet," warned John.

The fierce yapping from the door made all heads turn. Dan had Pooh-Bah on a short lead and held him tightly to heel, but Pooh-Bah wanted a fight. Bernie, too, was on his feet now, snarling a warning.

"Pooh-Bah! QUIET!" Bob's voice rapped out like a gunshot, and he stood tall over the angry dog. Pooh-Bah shrank to a sullen growling.

"And you can stop it, too," said Bob, with a glare at Bernie.

At Bob's next instruction, dogs and owners formed a circle and began to walk round, keeping their dogs to heel, praising and encouraging. Neil could see that Bob was keeping the two warring dogs apart. Dan and John were working hard to keep their dogs' attention on themselves and not on each other. So far, it was working.

"Tell your dogs to sit," said Bob, "and stay in the circle, facing inwards, with your dog on your left."

Neil knew what was coming. This could be touch and go.

"Neil," called Bob, "weave Jake in and out, please."

Neil nodded quickly and patted his leg, looking down into Jake's alert face. It was important to keep eye contact and hold Jake's attention as they wove in and out of the circle, behind one dog and its owner, in front of the

97

next. If Jake sniffed another dog, Neil called his name and gave the lead a little tug, just to keep his mind on what he was doing. Scrap tried to follow him, but was gently restrained by Toby.

"Good boy, Jake. That'll do." In heartfelt relief Neil knelt to pat Jake and tell him he was wonderful. Now it was another dog's turn, then Scrap's, then Pooh-Bah's.

"Keep talking to him, Dan," advised Bob.

Pooh-Bah trotted confidently in and out of the circle, his eyes on Dan's face. Neil's fists clenched as the Peke drew nearer to Bernie, but Dan kept talking and held his dog's attention.

Bernie didn't even raise his head as Pooh-Bah passed him. Dan, still talking, shortened his lead. Pooh-Bah walked obediently round the St Bernard.

But then, with a sudden twist, a snarl and a flurry of fur, Pooh-Bah rounded on Bernie. Bernie responded with a warning bark.

"Keep going!" called Bob. Dan, with Pooh-Bah tightly controlled on the lead, pulled him away and finished the walk to a round of applause.

"Well done, Dan," said Bob. "Let's try Bernie now."

Bernie plodded wearily round the ring. There

was just a menacing growl from Pooh-Bah as he passed him, which Bernie hardly appeared to notice.

"I don't think we'll try that off the lead today," laughed Bob. "But the more they do that exercise, the more they'll get used to it, and to each other. We'll do 'stay and recall' next."

After class, Neil and Emily always liked to meet the dogs. They were with Dan and Pooh-Bah when Bob joined them.

"Patience and practice, Dan, I'm sure that's what we need," he said. "How's the work coming on at the Jepsons'?"

Dan grimaced. "Sooner it's finished, the better, if you ask me. Mrs Jepson's always checking up on us and stopping us from getting on with the job, and then she complains that we're too slow. I can't be finished soon enough. Pooh-Bah doesn't like it."

"Do you always take him with you?" asked Emily. Pooh-Bah had often been there when Dan was building the rescue centre at King Street.

"On most jobs I do, but I can't on this one. You've met Sugar and Spice, haven't you? When they see Pooh-Bah they start yapping fit to burst, and they can keep it up for hours, so

I'm not allowed to bring him near the house."

"So what happens when you're at work?" asked Neil.

"He stays home, and I go back at lunchtime to take him out. My sister calls during the day to check he's OK, but it's not the same. He's used to being with me."

"That's it, then!" said Neil. "I said it must be anxiety! He's worried and stressed out!"

"And he's taking it out on Bernie?" said Bob. "You could be right, Neil. He may be just bored and miserable, and that's what makes him bad-tempered."

As they spoke, John led Bernie past. Pooh-Bah sprang, and snapped. There was a roaring growl from Bernie, and he hurled his weight at Pooh-Bah as both owners heaved on the leads – but there was no need. Pooh-Bah had already rolled over. Bob laughed.

"Not such a fighter now!" he smiled. "He knows he's not on his own territory, and not fighting to take over Bernie's, either. I'm sure he'll behave better when he's able to go to work with you again."

"Can't come soon enough," said Dan. "By the way, you know that dog show they're having in the park next weekend?"

"Yes, a few of our regulars are in it."

"Well, Mrs Jepson's entered Sugar and Spice in the obedience class."

"She's done what?" said Bob.

Emily nearly fell over laughing and Neil, tickling Jake's tummy, suddenly remembered that he hadn't posted Bev's letter withdrawing Milly from the competition. He thought for a moment and decided that he certainly wasn't going to post it now.

He'd had an idea.

Arriving home from school the next day, Neil put his bike away and hurried to the rescue centre. Emily was there, with Bob, Kate, and Bev with Milly in her arms.

"How's she doing?" asked Neil.

"She walked a bit further today. I hope she doesn't wear herself out. I'll just put her in her basket, then I'll start doing the feeding bowls for the boarding dogs."

"You won't," grinned Kate. "Carole and I are doing them."

Bev looked at the rota on the wall. "But . . ." she began.

"You're coming with us," smiled Bob, picking up the car keys. "In the car, everyone."

"Including Milly?" asked Bev uncertainly.

"Especially Milly," said Neil, and decided to put off explaining anything until the Range Rover was moving and it was too late for Bev to object. As they took the road to Old Padsham Emily took the lead, and told Bev about Will Hammick's invitation.

"We couldn't disappoint him," she said persuasively. "He wants so much to meet Milly."

"I suppose," sighed Bev, "it won't hurt Milly just to meet Mara. But she can't be expected to race around the garden."

As Bob drove, Emily read out the directions to Forge Cottage, Old Padsham. A short, rough track led to a small stone house with a fenced-off garden at the front. A polythene tunnel lay on the grass, with an upturned crate and a low jump made of a pole supported on bricks.

As soon as the Range Rover stopped, Milly sat up sharply. Her ears were pricked and her tail wagged quickly in anticipation. Bev put her lead on before lifting her down from the van.

"There must be more dogs here than just Mara," said Bev, getting out of the Range Rover. "A dog with three legs couldn't use that lot."

Excited barking grew louder as the front door opened. Barking and bounding from the house came a small, curly-coated, tan spaniel, galloping on three legs to meet them. Neil and Emily knelt to greet her and she leapt at them with a brief lick, but she was more interested in Milly. They sniffed and circled one another, Bev keeping Milly on a short lead and bending to protect her as she backed away nervously.

A small, middle-aged man with receding curly grey hair was walking towards them. He whistled to the spaniel, who scampered to his side.

"Hello, I'm Will Hammick," he called. "Best let your dog off the lead, then she won't feel threatened."

He extended a hand to Bev to shake. She

began to introduce the Parkers, but there was a smile of recognition.

"I've seen you all at dog shows. And this is the famous Milly of the website!" He knelt and held out his hands to Milly. She sniffed, wagged her tail, and went back to making friends with Mara. Bev frowned with anxiety.

"She'll be all right," Will reassured her. "Mara won't hurt her."

"Maybe, but she might hurt herself," said Bev. "She hasn't had the stitches out long."

"I know, but if she's an adventurous little monkey like Mara there'll be no stopping her," Will pointed out.

"How did Mara lose her leg?" asked Neil.

"It was in a road accident," said Will. "I was just walking her along one of these quiet little lanes when some boy racer came round the blind bend too fast and she bolted. Pity she didn't run the other way. You can't always protect them."

As Will spoke, Bev had slipped off Milly's lead and watched to see what would happen. Milly was investigating the tunnel.

"She'll go in one end and out at the other, no harm in that," smiled Will. Mara, who seemed to be showing off to her new friend, had dashed through three times already.

"I was training her for agility before her accident," he said. "She was a natural, always jumping, climbing, in and out of everything, more like a cat than a dog. It's a game, isn't it, Mara?"

Mara took a good run at the jump, changed her mind and ran round in a circle to approach the jump again. This time she cleared it with her curly black ears lifting as she stretched in mid air. Neil couldn't believe he was watching a three-legged dog. With another leap she landed on the box.

Cautiously, Milly inspected the jump. She ran at it, pushed her nose under, tried to crawl underneath it, couldn't, and shuffled out backwards as everyone laughed. Neil realized that Bev was laughing too – for the first time since Milly's accident. Milly put both front paws on the box and barked as Mara jumped down and raced away.

"Milly can't keep up," said Emily.

"Wait and see," said Will. "Once she's built up her strength again, she'll be as good as Mara. And Milly wants to succeed. You can tell that just looking at her."

They watched as Milly attempted to do

everything that Mara did. She didn't clear the jump or get onto the box, but she was having fun trying.

"She's had enough for one day," said Bev at last. "Come on, Milly!"

"You'll come again, I hope?" smiled Will.

Bev smiled. "Yes, I think we will. And thanks."

Neil and Emily exchanged a glance of triumph. Neil couldn't wait to put this on the website.

"I'll drop you off at home, Bev," said Bob, as they piled into the Range Rover. "Good to meet you, Will."

Neil put his arm round Milly as she sat bolt upright at the window, her head tilted, her bright eyes still watching Mara. Her paws were damp, there was grass in her coat, and she was happy. So was he.

As they reached Bev's house, Bev was bending over Milly and praising her, but when they parked, she looked up. Her smile vanished. Betty was on the doorstep.

Chapter Ten

"Don't worry," said Bob. "We'll come in with you." As Neil jumped down from the Range Rover, Betty turned and walked with difficulty to meet them.

"She's smiling!" he said. Milly pulled at the lead in her eagerness to greet Betty and lick the outstretched hands.

"Milly!" cried Betty. "You look so well! Bev!" She took Bev by the shoulders and kissed her. Neil and Emily stared in amazement.

"Does she have an identical twin?" whispered Emily.

"I'm sorry," Betty was saying. "I've been unkind about all this, but I was worried about poor Milly."

"Forget it," said Bev. "Come in. Look, Milly's thrilled to see you!"

Bob gave Betty his arm as they walked up the path, but Neil hung back.

"What are you staring at, Neil?" asked Bob.

"That's Sean Appleby's car, parked on the other side. But I can't see Fergus."

"Who's Fergus?" asked Emily, then gasped. "Wow! What a dog!"

Sean and Fergus were emerging from the park. Sean waved, and headed for the car with Fergus.

"Bring him in!" called Bev, but Sean shook his head.

"He's soaking," he called, bundling a very wet, muddy dog into the car. Then he ran over to join them. "Can't take him anywhere like that. Hi – you must be Bob Parker?"

"Dad!" prompted Neil, and Emily giggled. Bob was staring at the car as if hypnotized.

"Yes – hello – pleased to meet you," he said vaguely, then pulled himself together and smiled broadly. "That dog is magnificent!"

"He's nothing but legs and cuddly toy when you get to know him," said Sean. He was carrying a cardboard box under one arm, and when they were all indoors he presented it to

Bev. In it were some squeaky toys, two bags of dry dog food and a box of biscuits. Neil squeaked a rubber ball for Milly and rolled it across the floor for her to chase.

"After I'd talked to Mrs Parker, I calmed down a bit," admitted Betty. "And that lovely piece in the *Compton News* really made me think. I suppose I still think of Milly as 'my dog'. I've never really let go of her. But it's time I faced it. She's your dog now, Bev."

"But she's your friend," said Neil. "That's what counts."

"She wants her bear," said Emily. "It's on the chair, I'll get it."

"She can get it herself," said Bev with confidence. "Don't try to help her." Milly set off, reached the chair and pulled the teddy down.

"I'd like to go home before it gets dark," said Betty, "And it soon will be. Those lights still need mending."

"We were talking about that," said Neil. "Me and Fergus – I mean, Sean. We want to make Compton more dog-friendly."

"I've been thinking about posters," said Sean. "Not leaving dogs in the car in summer, getting them treated for fleas, that sort of thing. Educating owners."

"You get posters like that in vets' waiting rooms," said Emily, "but if you're at the vet's, it probably means that you care about animals anyway. They need to be where everyone can see them."

"For posters to be effective," said Sean, "they need to be big, they need to be bright, and they need to be everywhere. It's an expensive business. We'd need money. We should really set up a fund."

"We can help, can't we, Dad?" said Neil.

"It's certainly a good idea," said Bob. "The rescue centre at King Street already has charitable status and we could organize something through that."

"Excellent news. But it needs a good name," advised Sean.

"Milly's famous," said Neil. "What about 'The Milly Fund'?"

"That's a great idea," said Sean. "I thoroughly approve!"

"I always said you were a star, Milly," said Bev, smiling down at her dog. "You know, Neil, I'm beginning to wish I hadn't withdrawn her from that competition. She'd be even more of a star if she did well, and I think she could. I'd like us to show what a three-legged dog can do."

"Um – Bev," said Neil. He could feel his face getting warm. "About that competition – I'm sorry – you gave me the letter to post, but—"

"Oh, Neil!" interrupted Bob. "You didn't forget to post Bev's letter, did you?" Then he laughed. "Never mind, it's easy to lose letters. Somebody gave me a letter of resignation last week. I can't think what I've done with it."

Bev was watching Neil closely. "I don't suppose you forgot on purpose, did you Neil?" She sighed. "I suppose I should be angry. But I'm not."

On the afternoon of the Dog Show, the Compton Town Park was chaotic with the voices of dogs and owners.

Neil and Emily sat in a corner of the main arena with Milly, waiting for the obedience class to start. Friends of King Street had turned out to see Milly – Dr Harvey was there with Finn and Sandy, Dave Thomas had brought Billy, and Gina Ward had Denny, the golden retriever with her. They'd already seen Scrap win his class for Best Puppy and Emily's best friend Julie Baker, wearing a fluffy jacket with her hair brushed over her eyes, had paraded Ben the Old English sheepdog round the ring and carried off the trophy for the Dog Most Like Its Owner.

By now, Milly looked bored with the whole proceedings. Even when Bev came to join them, Milly only gave a token tail-wag and went back to sleep.

"I've been checking out the competition," she said, and she seemed nervous. "I don't think we should worry too much about Sugar and Spice. Bernie's here."

"Not Pooh-Bah?" asked Emily.

"No, Dan's working on a new job today and Pooh-Bah's with him. I don't know the others. I don't really care if Milly wins or not. I just want her to show what she can do." She knelt down beside her dog. "She's looking tired. I hope she's all right."

"Don't start that again!" said Neil. "I think the class is about to start."

"Bev, are you all right?" asked Emily.

"Yes, of course," she said, then, "no, I'm too tense for this. With everything that's happened, I'm as wound up as a clockwork mouse."

"It's nothing to worry about!" said Emily.

"I know, but I can't help it. I'm so keyed up, I'll upset Milly. If the owner is nervous, so is the dog. Neil, can you do it, please?"

"What – take Milly through her obedience class?"

"She knows you, Neil, she'll be fine with you. And you've done this so many times before. Will you take her?"

Neil knelt down and hugged Milly.

"I'd love to," he said. "Come on, then, star. Let's show them!"

Whatever obedience Sugar and Spice might have done, they had forgotten it as soon as they were surrounded by other dogs. Mr and Mrs Jepson coaxed and called them until their faces were as pink as Mrs Jepson's sweater, but Sugar and Spice were only interested in snapping at the opposition and finally had to be hauled from the room in disgrace.

When it was the turn of Milly and Neil to step up and start the course, the crowd suddenly went very quiet. Neil guessed that they knew what a special performance Milly was about to give.

Milly began slowly, cautiously following Neil's firm instructions and guiding movements. She walked the course with confidence and pride.

She sat, lay and stood – all at the word of Neil's command, her eyes fixed on his face, her ears pricked for every instruction.

So far she hadn't put a paw wrong.

She's enjoying this, thought Neil. *More than any other dog in this room, she's having fun.*

Finally, she trotted lopsidedly up to him, circled him, sat down at his heel and looked lovingly up into his face. "That'll do," said Neil softly, and patted her as wild applause for Milly broke out around the hall.

"What about that, then, cleverpaws?" said Emily, holding out her arms as Neil led Milly back to her place.

"I think she just wants her Christmas Bear!" said Neil. "Bev, here's Jake Fielding waiting for photographs."

"And here's Mum," said Emily. "Mum, you should have seen Milly! She was brilliant!"

"Of course she was!" said Carole. As she bent to fuss Milly, Neil saw that she had a sealed envelope in her hand. She passed it to him. "That came for you today. It looks interesting."

It certainly did. It had a bright logo and *Dogs and Superdogs* on the front. Neil ripped it open.

"Oh, this is class! Mum, Em, listen! They've been following my website diary, and they love it! They want to publish it in their magazine!"

"Well done!" said Carole.

"It's not me, it's Milly," said Neil, glancing towards Bev who was lost in smothering her dog with hugs and affection. Nobody else mattered to Bev right then. Just Milly. "It's her story," said Neil. "And I haven't finished it yet."

Later that night at King Street Kennels, Neil sat down at the office computer and began to type. Emily was sitting beside him.

Today, even though she didn't win, Milly showed us what she's made of, he began. He typed in his account of the dog show, and finished: *She's no longer young, and she's getting by on three legs, but she loves life and this hasn't beaten her.*

"Not bad," conceded Emily. "But you'll need a title. What are you going to call it?"

"Just wait," grinned Neil, and returned to the beginning of the diary. At the top of the screen, in bold capitals, he typed:

MILLY'S TRIUMPH

Look out for Puppy Patrol No. 11:

Perfect Puppy

Is she too good to be true?

Lucky is King Street Kennels' newest visitor, and she looks like the perfect puppy. Her cheeky charm soon wins her heaps of friends – including little Sarah Parker.

But Lucky isn't as perfect as she looks – in fact, she's a seriously strange pup. And when she leaves King Street, Neil and Emily learn that this beautiful puppy is hiding a dangerous secret . . .

Look out for Puppy Patrol No. 12:

Sam & Delilah

No one can keep them apart . . .

Delilah is Neil and Emily's new canine neighbour. She's a pedigree border collie and the apple of her owner's eye. And the Parkers' pet, Sam, has taken a shine to her.

But Delilah's owners are determined to keep them apart – they don't think Sam is good enough for their pedigree pooch. Can they stop a match made in doggie heaven?

Look out for Puppy Patrol No. 22:

Superdog!

Simply the best!

Superdog is a brand new competition for dogs of all shapes and sizes. And Twister is a natural winner. He's fast, he's clever, he's adorable – and Neil and Emily think he's top dog.

But it's tough at the top, and Twister faces stiff competition – from some very determined dog-owners. Can the Parkers help Twister prove that he really is the best?

Look out for Puppy Patrol No. 23:

Sherlock's Home

Will he make the grade?

Sherlock is strong, intelligent and reliable – perfect qualities for a would-be police dog. But there's one problem – his owner is an ex-thief!

When Sergeant Moorhead begins his search for a new dog, it's up to Neil and Emily Parker to persuade him that Sherlock is the right dog for the job . . .

PUPPY PATROL titles available from
Macmillan Children's Books

The prices shown below are correct at the time of going to press. However, Macmillan Publishers reserve the right to show new retail prices on covers which may differ from those previously advertised.

JENNY DALE

1. Teacher's Pet	0 330 34905 8	£2.99
2. Big Ben	0 330 34906 6	£2.99
3. Abandoned!	0 330 34907 4	£2.99
4. Double Trouble	0 330 34908 2	£2.99
5. Star Paws	0 330 34909 0	£2.99
6. Tug of Love	0 330 34910 4	£2.99
7. Saving Skye	0 330 35492 2	£2.99
8. Tuff's Luck	0 330 35493 0	£2.99
9. Red Alert	0 330 36937 7	£2.99
10. The Great Escape	0 330 36938 5	£2.99
11. Perfect Puppy	0 330 36939 3	£2.99
12. Sam and Delilah	0 330 36940 7	£2.99
13. The Sea Dog	0 330 37039 1	£2.99
14. Puppy School	0 330 37040 5	£2.99
15. A Winter's Tale	0 330 37041 3	£2.99
16. Puppy Love	0 330 37042 1	£2.99
17. Best of Friends	0 330 37043 X	£2.99
18. King of the Castle	0 330 37392 7	£2.99
19. Posh Pup	0 330 37393 5	£2.99
20. Charlie's Choice	0 330 37394 3	£2.99
21. The Puppy Project	0 330 37632 2	£2.99
22. Superdog!	0 330 37633 0	£2.99
23. Sherlock's Home	0 330 37634 9	£2.99
24. Forever Sam	0 330 37635 7	£2.99
25. Milly's Triumph	0 330 39087 2	£2.99
26. The Snow Dog	0 330 39088 0	£2.99

All Macmillan titles can be ordered at your local bookshop or are available by post from:

Book Service by Post
PO Box 29, Douglas, Isle of Man IM99 1BQ

Credit cards accepted. For details:
Telephone: 01624 675137
Fax: 01624 670923
E-mail: bookshop@enterprise.net

Free postage and packing in the UK.
Overseas customers: add £1 per book (paperback)
and £3 per book (hardback).